headwork reading

Slow Motion

and **Dead Weight**

Chris Culshaw

ty Press

Slow Motion

1

Into Thin Air

Mrs Robinson lifted her daughter Katy on to the roundabout. 'Daddy and I are going to have a cup of tea,' she said. 'We'll be just over there, in the café.'

The roundabout was crowded. Katy was sitting on a large silver horse. The ride started moving and she waved to her mother. Soon the ride was a blur of colour and noise. Mr Robinson said, 'It's going a bit fast. Are you sure it's safe, Brenda?'

His wife laughed, 'Safe as houses! I used to go on it when I was a girl. Don't be such an old fuss pot, Colin. Come on, I'm dying for a cuppa.' Colin Robinson tried to spot Katy's fair hair and bright red coat, but the ride was going too fast.

Five minutes later they were standing with the other parents waiting for the ride to stop. As the ride slowed down, Mr Robinson put his hand on his wife's arm. 'Where is she?' he said, 'Where's our Katy?' He could not see her.

'She must be on the other side,' said Mrs Robinson. But when the silver horse came into view it was empty!

2
Facts not Fiction

Two days later Katy Robinson was still missing. The police held a press conference. Inspector Reed spoke first: 'Good afternoon. My name is Tom Reed. I'm the officer in charge of this case. Now, there are lot of silly stories going around about Katy Robinson's disappearance.'

He gave the reporters a long hard look. 'It will help me, and Mr and Mrs Robinson, if we all stick to the facts.' He turned to a large map on the wall. 'Now, what are the facts? Katy's been missing for two days.' He pointed to the map: 'She was last seen here, in Ripton Park. A number of officers have searched the ride itself and the park. Nothing. Not a dicky bird. She must have got off that ride without anyone seeing her. But we've no idea how.'

Next Colin Robinson spoke. He held up a poster with Katy's picture on it. 'These have been put up all over town,' he said. He looked at the TV cameras. 'If you've seen our Katy...' He held the poster towards the cameras. He was shaking and could not hold the poster still. Brenda Robinson took it from him and said, 'We just want her back. That's all.'

3
What If?

The next day Mr Robinson rang Inspector Reed. 'Any news, Tom?'

'No, nothing,' said the Inspector, 'but I've had an idea. You know that the ride has been closed since Katy disappeared? Well, I want to open it again tomorrow night. We'll try to set everything up just as it was when Katy disappeared. We'll stage a reconstruction.'

'But why?' asked Mr Robinson. 'What good will that do?'

'It might help people to remember. It's worth a try, Colin.'

Mr Robinson agreed that anything was worth a try.

Inspector Reed said, 'I know it will be hard for you, and Mrs Robinson, but can you come too?'

'Of course. We'll be there.'

The police opened the ride at seven the next evening. This was the time Katy had disappeared. The park was quite busy. Two TV crews were there and some reporters.

When Mr and Mrs Robinson arrived, Inspector Reed was waiting near the roundabout. Next to him was a little girl who was about the same age as Katy. She had fair hair and was wearing a bright red coat.

Inspector Reed said, 'This is my niece, Polly. She's agreed to help us. She's going to ride on the silver horse...'

Mrs Robinson, shocked, said, 'No! She mustn't.'

Inspector Reed said, 'Mrs Robinson, listen to me, please. There are many people here tonight who were here when Katy went missing. Seeing Polly might help them to remember.'

She looked at her husband, 'Colin, please. What if...?'

The policeman smiled, 'What can go wrong?

I've got officers all over the park. The owner ran the ride a few minutes just before you came. It's in perfect working order. He's going to run it at half speed – for just a few minutes.' He turned to his niece, 'You can handle that, can't you, Pol?'

The little girl grinned at her uncle. Inspector Reed patted her on the head.

Mrs Robinson bent down and spoke very quietly to Polly: 'Are you sure you want to do this, Polly? All by yourself?'

The girl nodded slowly, 'Yes. If it'll help find your Katy.'

4
Out of Control

Polly felt very important as she sat on the big silver horse and waited for the ride to start. A roundabout all to herself. TV cameras and reporters. She could not wait to tell her friends.

The controls for the ride were in a little hut next to the café. Inspector Reed stood next to the owner.

The roundabout started to turn very slowly. Mr Robinson had to look away. The pain of remembering was like a hammer blow to his heart. His wife stood perfectly still, as still as the watching statues in the park.

Suddenly, without warning, the ride started to speed up. Mrs Robinson heard Inspector Reed shouting at the owner, 'I said half speed. Stop it right now!'

The owner tried to stop the ride, but could not. Tom Reed grabbed the controls but he could not stop it either. He ran over towards the ride. It was spinning like a top now. 'Polly!' he shouted. He started to panic. He could not see the horse or his niece.

Colin Robinson ran to his side, 'I thought you said...'

The policeman did not answer. He started to run alongside the ride. He was going to jump on to it! Mrs Robinson screamed, 'No! You'll kill yourself!'

5
If Only...

The TV news later that night told the whole story. Polly waving and smiling. That sudden murderous burst of speed. Tom Reed throwing himself at the ride and then falling – dead – at Colin Robinson's feet. Police officers rushing about. Panic. Then the ride slowing down. Stopping. The horror on Brenda Robinson's face, seeing the silver horse – empty.

During the next few awful days, Brenda and Colin felt as if they were riding a whirlwind. Reporters at their door, day and night. Tom Reed's funeral. Meeting Polly's parents. Not knowing what to say to them. Blaming themselves. If only they had not taken Katy to the park. If only they had not allowed Polly to go on the ride. If only... if only...

Brenda Robinson went back to the park every day. She refused to believe that her daughter or Polly were dead. The roundabout was boarded up. The police arrested the owner that week, but let him go the next day. As far as they could see, the ride was in perfect working order.

6
A Phone Call

About a week after Tom Reed's death, Mr and Mrs Robinson got a call from a reporter called Maggie Mort who worked for the local paper. 'Can we meet?' she said. 'There's something I think you should see.' They went to see her the same day.

'I want you to have a look at this video tape,' she said and switched on a TV. 'It's the tape that was made the night Tom Reed was killed.'

Colin could hardly bear to look at it again. Brenda sat, very still, looking, looking...

The tape finished. Brenda wiped her eyes. 'I don't understand,' she said to Maggie. 'There's nothing...'

Maggie rewound the tape, 'This time I'll play it in slow motion. This is a special tape machine. It slows the film right down.'

7
Burn It!

Very slowly, as if she is deep under water, a little girl gets on a silver horse. The ride starts to turn. Very slowly, like the Earth turning its face to the Sun. Faster now. A sudden flash of silver. A horse's hoof. A man falling. Faster now. A red coat. Fair hair blowing. 'Now,' whispered Maggie, 'look at the hair.'

Polly's hair turned grey! Colin stood up and shouted, 'Oh my God! Switch it off! I don't want to see any more!

But Brenda said quietly, 'No. Let it run.'

The grey hair blew away. Polly's face had aged a hundred years. Her skin flaked off like bark. Her head was a screaming skull. Then, as they watched in horror, she blew away, like the seeds of a dandelion clock.

Maggie Mort stopped the machine, took out the tape and gave it to Mrs Robinson.

Brenda looked at her, searching her face for the answer to the question they both knew had to be asked. At last she asked it: 'Will you write about this in your paper?'

The young reporter smiled a slow, sad smile. 'I want to. It would make my name. I'll probably never find a better story.' She looked across at Colin, his tired face, his red-ringed eyes. 'But I won't. If Katy or Polly were my daughter...'

Colin reached out and touched Maggie's arm. 'Thank you,' he said.

Brenda looked at the tape. 'What shall we do with this?'

'Burn it,' said Maggie Mort, 'burn it.'

'Burn it,' repeated Colin.

8
Awake or Dreaming?

Because of the TV and newspaper reports, Mr and Mrs Robinson got lots of phone calls and letters. Most people were kind. Some were from people who had themselves lost children, through accidents or illness. Some were from sick, wicked people. Brenda made sure Colin did not see these letters. He was not as strong as she was.

About a week after their meeting with Maggie Mort, Brenda received this note:

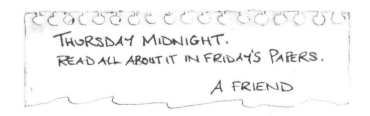

THURSDAY MIDNIGHT.
READ ALL ABOUT IT IN FRIDAY'S PAPERS.

A FRIEND

She threw the note in the fire and forgot all about it until the next night. She was in the kitchen by herself. Colin had gone upstairs to bed. She opened the local newpaper and there, on page 2, she read:

The roundabout in Ripton Park, linked to the disappearance of two local young girls, Katy Robinson and Polly Reed, burned down last night. Police think the fire was started deliberately.

She ran upstairs with the paper and found Colin asleep. She shook him gently, but he was in a very deep sleep. It was the first time he had slept, really slept, since they had lost Katy. As she looked down at his face – peaceful at last – Brenda Robinson knew who had started the fire. But she never spoke about it again and neither did Colin.

Dead Weight

It was nine o'clock on 27 April 1994. Inspector Karen Harmer, Head of Withershaw CID, had just arrived at her office. There was a letter on her desk. She opened it and read this.

To the Head of CID
Withershaw Police

By the time you read this a man will be dead. And his killer too. I know what I am going to do is wrong. I know two wrongs don't make a right. But we both deserve to die. And now I've started I can't stop. Something is driving me on. It's like being on a roller-coaster.

You know the man I'm going to kill. Everyone in Withershaw knows him. You'll find out who I am, soon enough. I'm on your files. But that doesn't matter. I'm already a dead man.

I need to tell you a bit about myself, so you will understand why I'm doing this. Last month I was told I had six weeks to live. Cancer: in the brain. There is nothing the doctors can do. Six weeks to live and all they could say was 'sorry'. I've got drugs to control the pain. They work – most of the time.

I've got no wife or kids. No other family. No real friends. Lots of money. Money to burn. I told the doctors I'd give them a million quid if they could give me another year. Six months. Even another six weeks.

I'm what they call a 'Wheeler Dealer' – a con man, if you prefer. I've made money in New York, Paris, Hong Kong, Rio. I've been all over the world.

So what has brought me to Withershaw? Well it's quite touching really! I came here with my dad when I was a kid, forty years ago, for the only real holiday we had before he died.

I booked in at the Royal Oak last Tuesday. It was early and the pub was very quiet. I sat down in a corner with my drink. Two women came in and sat near me. They didn't seem to notice me. One, a middle-aged woman with red hair, was very angry about something. She was holding a newspaper and pointing to a picture on the front page. She said to the other woman, 'Someone's going to murder Howard one of these days! It's time your newspaper told the truth about him.'

The other woman – she was obviously a reporter – took out a note pad. The red-haired woman started to tell her about this man Howard. Her husband used to work for him. She said he was a snake. He'd made millions by cheating and lying. And worse still, she said, he arranged for people to 'disappear'. He'd had people killed. Her own husband was one of them. Drowned while he was fishing. The reporter asked her why.

Howard had had her husband killed, said the woman, because he knew too much. When she told him she'd go to the police, he said that if she did one of her children might just be involved in an 'accident'. The woman was very angry. The reporter looked across at me and told the woman to keep her voice down. He was like a cancer, the red-haired woman went on. He was a ruthless, violent man. Yet there he was on the front page of the local paper. He was acting like Father Christmas, handing over money to a children's home.

The more she talked, the more angry she became. In the end, she was shaking with rage. And what she said made me feel sick. You see, she could have been talking about me. I'm just like Howard. Just as ruthless. I have lied and cheated. I've used bullies to frighten women and kids. I've never killed anyone myself, though. Not yet.

The red-haired woman asked the reporter to help her. The reporter shook her head. She must have proof. She couldn't say Howard was a killer – not without proof. The reporter had heard lots of stories about Howard. She said lots of people in Withershaw wanted to see him behind bars. Or dead.

At that moment I made up my mind to do something about Howard. But first I wanted to be sure that the red-haired woman was telling the truth. I wanted to be sure he was as guilty as me.

It was easy. All you need is a good private detective and plenty of money and you can find out anything you want, about almost anybody. The woman was right. Half of Whithershaw had it in for Howard. Everyone was scared of him. But not me.

I discovered that Howard goes fishing every morning. He's a fishing fanatic. A man called Rogers takes him out in a rubber dinghy. They go out two or three miles to the old lighthouse.

Getting to know Rogers was easy. He'll talk to anyone who will buy him a drink. I told him I wanted to meet Howard. I said I was trying to set up a deal with him – a very private deal. Rogers did not seem surprised when I offered him £500 to fix it so that I could meet Howard alone.

It was so simple. Rogers phoned Howard. He said he was sick and was unable to take him fishing tomorrow. But he'd asked a 'mate' to stand in for him. Howard didn't mind. All he wanted was someone to steer the inflatable.

Well, it's time. In ten minutes I'll be meeting Howard at the harbour. I've got everything I need – handcuffs, sharp knife. I hope I can go through with it. I'm writing this letter so you'll know that nobody else is involved. Just me. Acting alone. Completely alone.

Inspector Harmer had just finished reading the letter when the station sergeant came into her office. He said, 'This has just come in from the local coastguard station, ma'am.' He dropped a message on her desk.

Two men found washed up on beach near Withershaw Head at 8am. One was dead. The other has been taken by helicopter to Witherby General Hospital.

The next day the front page of the local paper carried this story:

Local Millionaire Drowns

The body of local businessman Robert Howard and that of another man, as yet unidentified, were washed up near Withershaw Head early yesterday morning.

The mystery man's wrist was fastened to Mr Howard's ankle by a pair of handcuffs. Doctors at Witherby General say he has a slim chance of surviving.

Both men were wearing life-jackets which appear to have been slashed with a sharp instrument. A rubber dinghy, washed up on the other side of Withershaw Head, had also been slashed.

The police officer in charge of the case, Inspector Karen Harmer, will make a full statement later today.

Oxford University Press, Great Clarendon Street,
Oxford, OX2 6DP

Oxford   New York
Athens   Auckland   Bangkok   Bogota   Bombay
Buenos Aires   Calcutta   Cape Town   Dar es Salaam
Delhi   Florence   Hong Kong   Istanbul   Karachi
Kuala Lumpur   Madras   Madrid   Melbourne
Mexico City   Nairobi   Paris   Singapore
Taipei   Tokyo   Toronto

and associated companies in
Berlin   Ibadan

Oxford is a trade mark of Oxford University Press

© Chris Culshaw 1995
First published 1995
Reprinted 1996, 1997

ISBN 0 19 833497 4

Printed in Great Britain

Illustrations by Alan Marks